D1278285

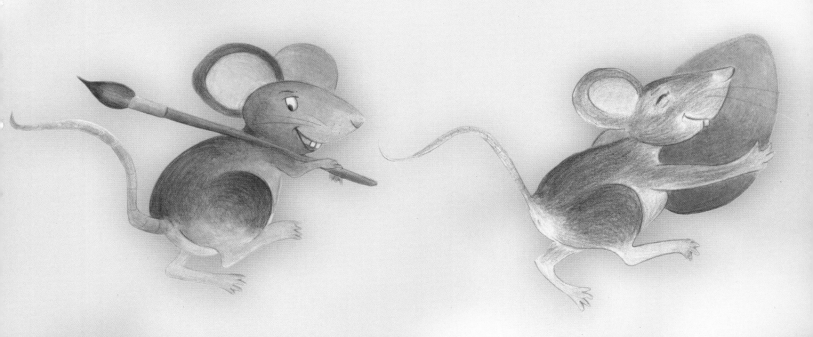

Easter Morning,
Easter Sun

Rosanna Battigelli • Tara Anderson

pajamapress

Easter morning,
Easter sun,

Easter breakfast,
Easter bun.

Easter bonnet,
Easter hats,

Easter flowers,
Easter cats!

Easter springtime,
Easter buzz,

Easter chirping,
Easter fuzz.

Easter hunting,
Easter seek,

Easter finding,
Easter peek.

Easter tumble,
Easter run,

Easter mishap,
Easter fun!

Easter helping,
Easter care,

Easter buddies,
Easter share.

Easter hopping,
Easter race,

Easter painting,
Easter face!

Easter carrot,
Easter bake,

Easter frosting,
Easter cake.

Easter knocking,
Easter guest,

Easter Bunny,
Easter best!

Easter dinner,
Easter pie,
Easter feasting,
Easter sigh.

Easter sunset,
Easter light,

Easter bedtime,
Easter night.

First published in Canada and the United States in 2021

Text copyright © 2021 Rosanna Battigelli
Illustration copyright © 2021 Tara Anderson
This edition copyright © 2021 Pajama Press Inc.
This is a first edition.

10 9 8 7 6 5 4 3 2 1

www.pajamapress.ca   info@pajamapress.ca

The publisher gratefully acknowledges the support of the Canada Council for the Arts and the Ontario Arts Council for its publishing program. We acknowledge the financial support of the Government of Canada through the Canada Book Fund (CBF) for our publishing activities.

Library and Archives Canada Cataloguing in Publication

Title: Easter morning, Easter sun / by Rosanna Battigelli ; illustrated by Tara Anderson.
Names: Battigelli, Rosanna, author. | Anderson, Tara, illustrator.
Identifiers: Canadiana 20200365541 | ISBN 9781772781779 (hardcover)
Classification: LCC PS8553.A8334 E27 2021 | DDC jC813/.54—dc23

Publisher Cataloging-in-Publication Data (U.S.)

Names: Battigelli, Rosanna, author. | Anderson, Tara, illustrator.
Title: Easter Morning, Easter Sun / by Rosanna Battigelli ; illustrated by Tara Anderson.
Description: Toronto, Ontario Canada : Pajama Press, 2021. | Summary: "From sunrise to bedtime, a family of cats celebrates Easter with a day full of traditions. These include fancy bonnets, hot cross buns for breakfast, an egg hunt, games in the meadow, and a special dinner together. Small upsets like a spilled Easter basket are lovingly resolved" -- Provided by publisher.
Identifiers: ISBN 978-1-77278-177-9 (hardcover)
Subjects: LCSH: Easter stories. | Cats – Juvenile fiction. | Stories in rhyme. | BISAC: JUVENILE FICTION / Holidays & Celebrations / Easter & Lent. | JUVENILE FICTION / Animals / Cats.
Classification: LCC PZ7.1B344Ea | DDC [E] – dc23

Cover and book design—Lorena Gonzalez Guillen

Printed in China by WKT Company

Pajama Press Inc.
469 Richmond St. E, Toronto, ON M5A 1R1

Distributed in Canada by UTP Distribution
5201 Dufferin Street Toronto, Ontario Canada, M3H 5T8

Distributed in the U.S. by Ingram Publisher Services
1 Ingram Blvd. La Vergne, TN 37086, USA

Original art created
with oil-based colored pencil
and mineral spirits

For my sweet little
granddaughter Rosalie, w
brings so much joy!
-R.B.

For my Mother, who alwa
believes in me
~T.A.

YOU CAN DECORATE
EASTER EGGS TOO!

YOU WILL NEED

An adult helper
Hard-boiled eggs
Newspaper
Hot water
Small bowls or mugs—one per color
White vinegar
Food coloring
A spoon
An empty egg carton

HOW TO

1. Cover your table with newspaper to protect it from stains.

2. Have your adult helper add one cup of hot water to each small bowl or mug.

3. For each bowl or mug, stir in fifteen drops of food coloring and one teaspoon of vinegar.

4. Use a spoon to dip the eggs in the dye mixture. For a pale color, leave them in for ten seconds. For a bright color, leave them in for two minutes.

5. To dry your eggs, rest them sideways across the holes of an egg carton.

These eggs are safe to eat as long as you use food-grade food coloring. If you are going to keep your eggs a while, store them in the refrigerator.